W9-CQG-098

CRABTREE CONTACT

TOP 10 SMALLEST

Ben Hubbard

The pygmy rattlesnake

🌳 Crabtree Publishing Company

www.crabtreebooks.com

Crabtree Publishing Company

www.crabtreebooks.com   1-800-387-7650

PMB 59051   616 Welland Avenue,
350 Fifth Avenue, 59th Floor St. Catharines, Ontario
New York, NY, 10118   L2M 5V6

Content development by   Published by
Shakespeare Squared   Crabtree Publishing
                             Company © 2010
www.ShakespeareSquared.com
                             First published
No part of this publication may in Great Britain in
be reproduced, copied, stored in 2010 by TickTock
a retrieval system or transmitted in Entertainment Ltd.
any form or by any means electronic,
mechanical, photocopying, recording Printed in the
or otherwise without prior written   U.S.A./122009
permission of the copyright owner.   CG20091120

Crabtree Publishing   TickTock credits:
Company credits: Publisher: Melissa Fairley
Project manager: Kathy Middleton Art director: Faith Booker
Editor: Reagan Miller   Editor: Victoria Garrard
Production coordinator: Katherine Berti Designer: Emma Randall
Prepress technician: Katherine Berti   Production controller: Ed Green
                             Production manager: Suzy Kelly

Thank you to Lorraine Petersen and the members of nasen

Picture credits (t=top; b=bottom; c=centre; l=left; r=right; OFC=outside front cover): AFP/Getty
Images: 5t, 18–19. Barry Bland/Barcroft Media Ltd: 22b. Andy Carter: 15c. Caters News
Agency Ltd/Rex Features: 27b, 29br. Mark Clifford/Barcroft Media Ltd: 5b, 20, 21, 29tr. Carl
Court/PA Archive/Press Association Images: 2, 14–15, 28br. Courtesy of Robin Starr: 10, 11b,
28tr. Courtesy of The Arizona Aerospace Foundation: 11t. Firebox.com: 4, 24, 29cl. Getty
Images: 23. Motoring Picture Library/Alamy: OFC. NHPA/James Carmichael Jr: 1, 16–17,
29tl. Ed Oudenaarden/epa/Corbis. Steven Schffner/Emporis: 6, 28tl. Shutterstock: 7, 13, 22t.
South West News Service/Rex Features: 16, 27tl. David Burner/Rex Features: 27tr. Takako
Uno: 12, 29bl. Wildlife GmbH/Alamy: 8–9, 29cr.

Every effort has been made to trace copyright holders, and we apologize in advance
for any omissions. We would be pleased to insert the appropriate acknowledgments
in any subsequent edition of this publication.

Library and Archives Canada Cataloguing in Publication

Hubbard, Ben
     Top 10 smallest / Ben Hubbard.

(Crabtree contact)
Includes index.
ISBN 978-0-7787-7491-4 (bound).--ISBN 978-0-7787-7512-6 (pbk.)

     1. Size perception--Juvenile literature.
I. Title. II. Title: Top ten smallest. III. Series: Crabtree contact

BF299.S5H83 2010   j153.7'52   C2009-906644-0

Library of Congress Cataloging-in-Publication Data

Hubbard, Ben.
  Top 10 smallest / Ben Hubbard.
      p. cm. -- (Crabtree contact)
  Includes index.
  ISBN 978-0-7787-7491-4 (reinforced lib. bd.g : alk. paper) --
ISBN 978-0-7787-7512-6 (pbk. : alk. paper)
  1. Size perception--Juvenile literature. I. Title. II. Series.

BF299.S5H8355 2010
152.14'2--dc22

                              2009045510

Peel P50

CONTENTS

INTRODUCTION

The world we live in is getting bigger, but much of what we love is small. Small things can be cool, clever, and cute.

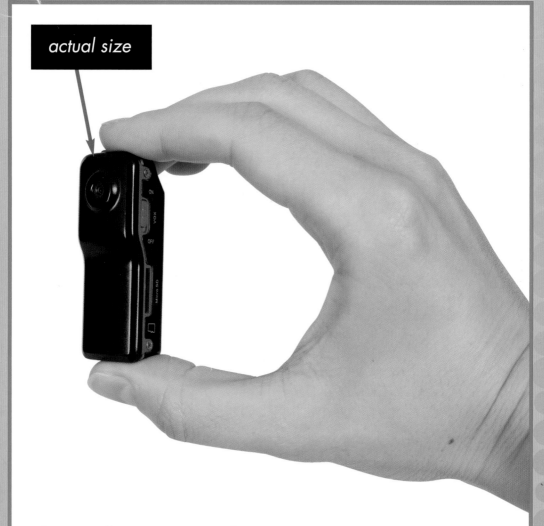

actual size

The smallest **camcorder** in the world is just 2.16 inches (5.5 centimeters) long.

The world's smallest helicopter can reach a speed of 62 miles per hour (100 kilometers an hour).

Mr. Peebles is the world's smallest cat. He is the same size as a guinea pig.

SMALLEST SKYSCRAPER

Skyscrapers **are the tallest buildings on Earth, but there is one that is surprisingly small.**

The smallest skyscraper was built in Texas in 1919.

It is said that a **con artist** designed it. He told the people buying it that it would be 40 stories high—instead it was only four! That is about 42.6 feet (13 meters) high.

Vatican City in Italy is the world's smallest country. It is home to the Pope.

It measures 0.16 square miles (0.44 square kilometers) and has a population of around 900 people.

The Vatican has its own government, police force, and even its own currency.

SMALLEST MAMMAL

The Etruscan pygmy shrew is the smallest mammal in the world.

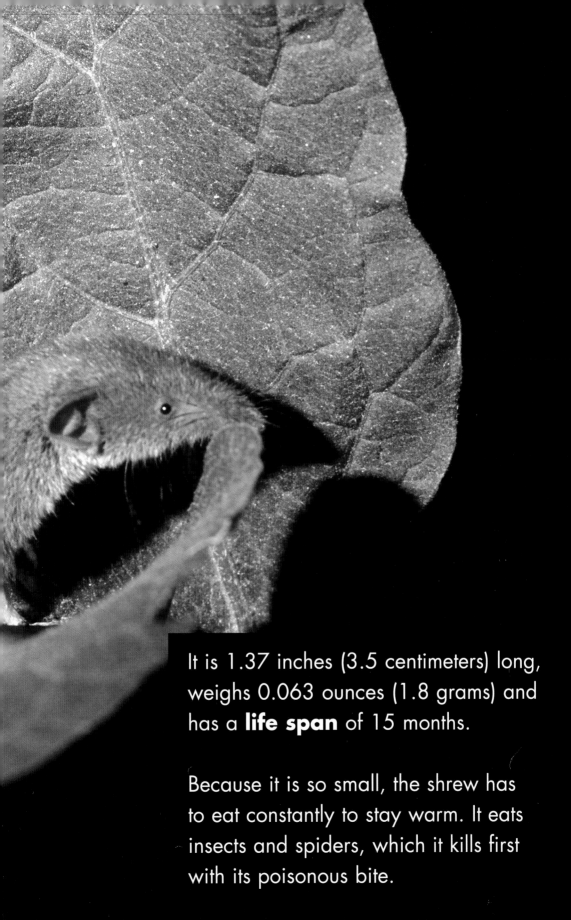

It is 1.37 inches (3.5 centimeters) long, weighs 0.063 ounces (1.8 grams) and has a **life span** of 15 months.

Because it is so small, the shrew has to eat constantly to stay warm. It eats insects and spiders, which it kills first with its poisonous bite.

SMALLEST PLANE

The smallest plane in the world was called Bumblebee II.

In 1984 Robert Starr built the Bumblebee to set the record for the smallest plane. But the record was soon broken by another plane, so Robert built the Bumblebee II in 1988.

Bumblebee

But on its first flight, Bumblebee II crashed! Robert was not injured, but the plane was destroyed. Luckily, he had flown Bumblebee II for enough time to set a new record.

Bumblebee II stats:
- length: 8.85 feet (2.7 meters)
- weight: 395.95 pounds (179.6 kilograms)
- **wingspan**: 5.57 feet (1.7 meters)
- top speed: 189.5 miles per hour (305 kilometers per hour)

Bumblebee II

SMALLEST SEAHORSE

Satomi's pygmy seahorse is only the size of your fingernail.

At 0.5 inches (13 millimeters) long it is the smallest seahorse in the world.

As with all seahorses, it is the males that become **pregnant**, not the females.

It is the same size as a fingernail.

A Satomi's pygmy seahorse baby is the size of a comma!

Seahorses vary greatly in size. The biggest can be up to 11.8 inches (30 centimeters) long.

SMALLEST CAR

The Peel P50 is the smallest car ever made.

The Peel P50 *parked in Piccadilly Circus, London*

It is designed to fit only one person. The car is 3.9 feet (1.2 meters) high and 4.2 feet (1.3 meters) long.

The *Peel P50* has no reverse gear. The driver has to get out of the car and use a special handle to lift the car up to turn it around.

handle for lifting car up by hand

The *Peel's* top speed is just 39.7 miles per hour (64 kilometers per hour).

SMALLEST RATTLESNAKE

The pygmy rattlesnake is only 17.7 inches (45 centimeters) long.

It uses its fangs to inject **venom** into its prey. Although not deadly to humans, its bite can make people very ill.

leaf

All rattlesnakes have **rattles** at the end of their tails. The pygmy's rattle is so small it sounds more like a soft "buzz."

rattle

SMALLEST HELICOPTER

Have you ever wished you could travel to school in a personal helicopter?

The GEN H-4 could be for you!

The GEN H-4 is the smallest **manned** helicopter in the world. It weighs 154.3 pounds (70 kilograms) and has a top speed of 55.9 miles per hour (90 kilometers per hour). From top to bottom it measures just 7.8 feet (2.4 meters).

It has two rotors, a chair, a footrest, and a handlebar. The handlebar is used to steer the helicopter forward, backward, left, or right.

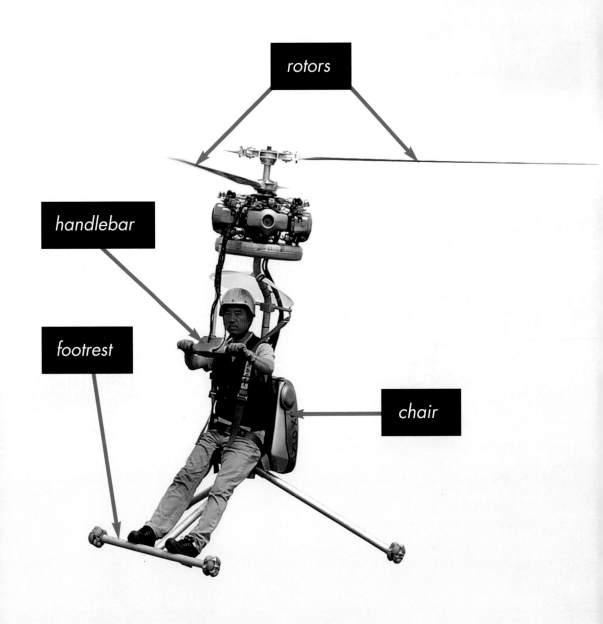

rotors

handlebar

footrest

chair

Just strap in and you are ready to go!

SMALLEST PET CAT

The smallest pet cat in the world is named Mr. Peebles.

At only 5.9 inches (15 centimeters) long and weighing 3.08 pounds (1.4 kilograms), Mr. Peebles can fit into a small glass.

A vet first noticed the cat during a visit to a farm. Everyone thought Mr. Peebles was just a kitten.

But on closer inspection the vet realized Mr. Peebles was a full-grown cat!

**Despite his size, Mr. Peebles
eats four meals a day.**

TINY PETS

Roborovski is the smallest type of hamster. They grow to just 1.96 inches (five centimeters) long.

Heaven Sent Brandy, a Chihuahua, is the smallest living dog. She is just six inches (15.2 centimeters) from nose to tail.

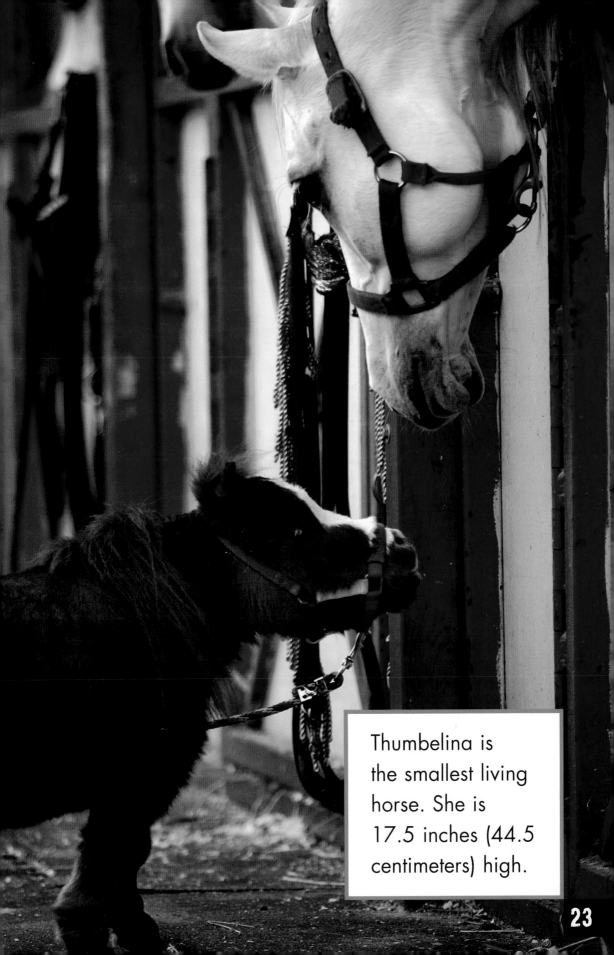

Thumbelina is the smallest living horse. She is 17.5 inches (44.5 centimeters) high.

SMALLEST CAMERA

Have you ever dreamed of becoming the next James Bond? Or perhaps a movie director?

The smallest camcorder in the world will come in handy for either.

record button

actual size

The Muvi™ Micro Camcorder is only 2.16 inches (5.5 centimeters) long, weighs 1.76 ounces (50 grams) and is small enough to hang around your neck.

The camera certainly isn't complicated to use. It only has one button—record.

The DelFly Micro is a tiny **remote-controlled** plane with a camera. It has a wingspan of just 3.9 inches (ten centimeters). **Guinness World Records™** lists it as the smallest camera plane.

The plane has a tiny battery on board which powers the plane for up to three minutes. Because of its size, the DelFly Micro can be used to take photos of difficult-to-reach or dangerous places.

DelFly Micro

SMALLEST SCULPTURES

Willard Wigan makes sculptures **so small you need a microscope to see them.**

The sculptures fit onto the head of a pin or into the eye of a needle.

Willard has used eyelashes as paintbrushes and even grains of sand to make his sculptures.

He says the hardest part is staying still long enough to work.

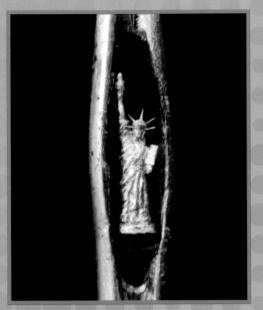

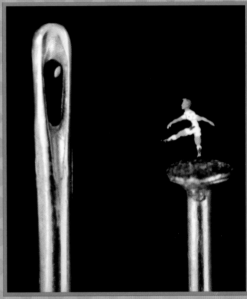

"Every movement I make is so small. I have to control my breathing and heartbeat; it's not easy."
Willard Wigan

TOP TEN SMALLEST

Some of the smallest things on Earth are created by nature. Others were built by humans.

They are all amazing record breakers.

10

Smallest skyscraper: LaSalle Street, Wichita Falls, Texas

42.6 feet (13 meters) high

9

Smallest plane: Bumblebee II

8.85 feet (2.7 meters) long

8

Smallest Helicopter: GEN H-4

7.8 feet (2.4 meters) high

7

Smallest car: Peel P50

4.2 feet (1.3 meters) long

6

Smallest rattlesnake:
Pygmy rattlesnake

17.7 inches
(45 centimeters) long

5

Smallest pet cat:
Mr. Peebles

5.9 inches
(15 centimeters) long

4

Smallest camera:
Muvi™ Micro Camcorder

2.16 inches
(5.5 centimeters) long

3

Smallest mammal:
Etruscan pygmy shrew

1.37 inches (3.5
centimeters) long

2

Smallest seahorse:
Satomi's pygmy seahorse

0.5 inches
(13 millimeters) long

1

Smallest sculptures:
Willard Wigan's sculptures

0.0002 inches
(0.005 millimeters)

camcorder
A lightweight, hand-held videocassette recorder

con artist Someone who cheats or tricks people by persuading them something is true, when it is not

Guinness World Records™
An organization that records and measures record-breaking things and events. The world records are then published in a book each year

life span The length of time a human or animal lives for

mammal An animal with fur or hair that gives birth to a live baby and feeds it with milk from its own body. A mammal's body temperature stays the same

manned When a human is on board or on site

pregnant Carrying unborn young inside the body

rattle Part of a snake that makes a quick knocking sound

remote-controlled
A device that is operated without the use of wires and from a distance

sculpture Art that is made in 3D, often carved out of stone, wood, or cast from metal or plaster

skyscraper A very tall building that tends to dominate a skyline

venom A powerful poison produced in the bodies of some animals, such as snakes and spiders

wingspan
A measurement from the tip of one wing to the tip of the other on a bird or airplane

SMALL FACTS

- The dwarf lantern shark is around 6.3 inches (16 centimeters) long. You could hold it in your hand, and it is reasonably harmless.

- Bonsai is the Japanese art of growing miniature trees. The smallest bonsais are called Keshi-tsubu and are less than one inch (2.5 centimeters) high.

- The smallest house in the world is in Amsterdam, Holland. It is just 3.28 feet (one meter) wide.

FIND OUT MORE ONLINE

www.willard-wigan.com
Learn more about Willard Wigan's art.

www.worldssmallesthorse.com
Find out more about Thumbelina, the world's smallest horse.

www.peel-cars-p50.co.uk/
See pictures and learn facts about the world's smallest car.

www.guinnessworldrecords.com
Learn more about Guinness World Records™.

Publisher's note to educators and parents:
Our editors have carefully reviewed these web sites to ensure that they are suitable for children. Many websites change frequently, however, and we cannot guarantee that a site's future contents will continue to meet our high standards of quality and educational value. Be advised that children should be closely supervised whenever they access the Internet.

INDEX